This Walker book belongs to:

_____

_____

_____

KEEP OUT

BEWARE

Private

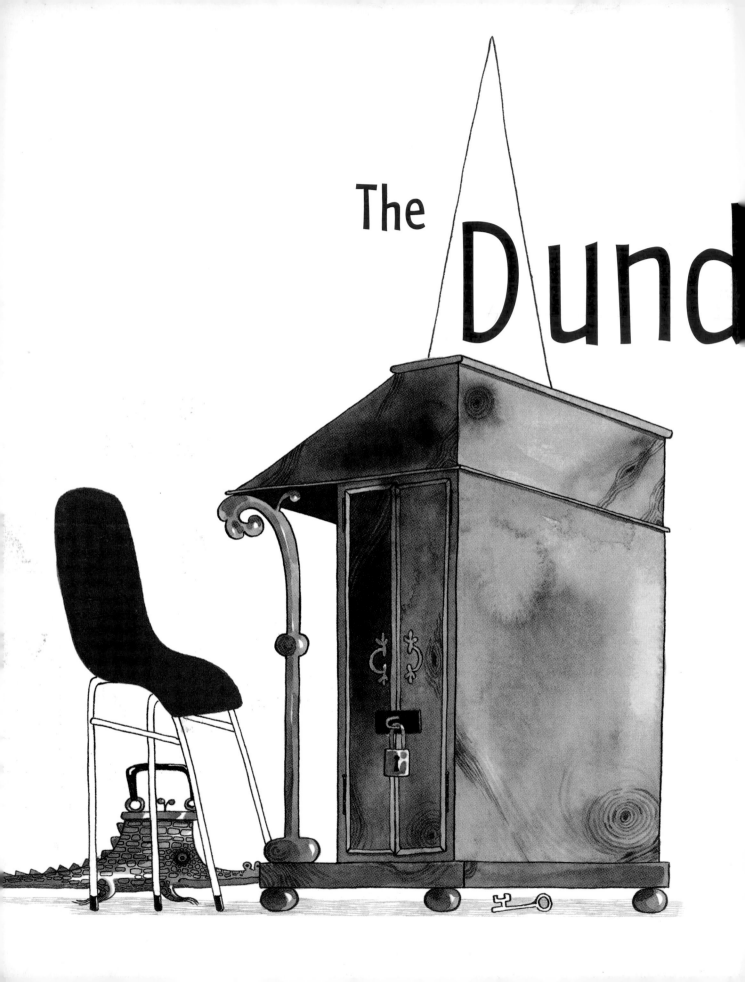

The Dund

erheads

PAUL FLEISCHMAN

illustrated by DAVID ROBERTS

WALKER BOOKS
AND SUBSIDIARIES

LONDON · BOSTON · SYDNEY · AUCKLAND

First published 2009 by Walker Books Ltd
87 Vauxhall Walk, London SE11 5HJ

This edition published 2010

2 4 6 8 10 9 7 5 3 1

This book has been typeset in Esprit.

Printed in China

British Library Cataloguing in Publication Data:
a catalogue record for this book is available from the British Library

ISBN 978-1-4063-2604-8

www.walker.co.uk

For Milton Love
P. F.

For Auntie Barbara
D. R.

"**Never,**" shrieked Miss Breakbone, "have I been asked to teach such a scraping-together of fiddling, twiddling, time-squandering, mind-wandering, doodling, dozing, don't-knowing **dunderheads!**"

That was her first mistake: the insult.
Mistake Number 2: no eye for talent.
An easy mistake to make, in our case.

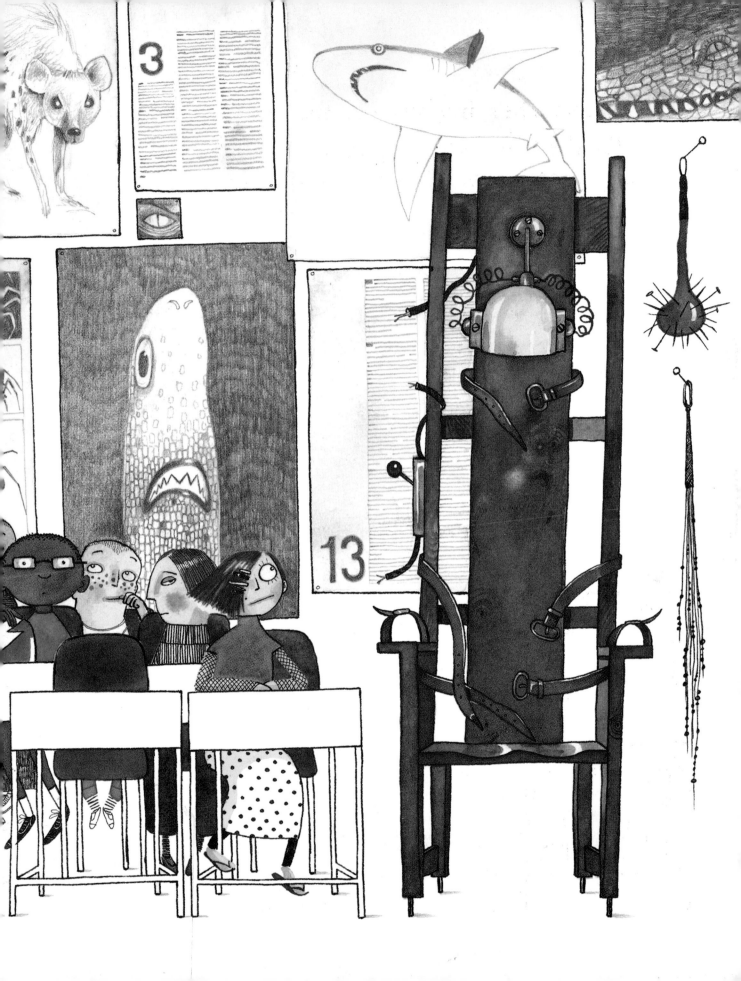

Miss Breakbone hated kids.
Every time she made a child
cry, she gave herself a gold star.

Confiscating was her speciality.

Rumour had it she bought her electric chair
from selling the stuff she'd taken away.

Then, one Friday, she went too far.

"Theodore!
Bring that
    magnifying
glass up
    here this
    instant!"

She didn't know that we all called him Junkyard, because he was always finding things in bins ...

like the one-eared cat he picked up on the way to school that morning. You should have seen his face light up.

His mother was mad about cats and he needed a present for her birthday on Sunday. It was perfect.

"And bring the cat!" snapped Miss Breakbone.
Mistake Number 3:
the outrage.

Junkyard put them both on her desk.
And then he started crying, in front of all the
girls. Miss Breakbone gave herself a gold star.
"But they're mine," Junkyard said.
"Not any more," snapped Miss Breakbone.
She studied the cat's strange green eyes with
interest. "And don't even *think* about getting
them back!"
Mistake Number 4: the dare.

She locked Junkyard's things in a drawer and smiled. Junkyard looked at me. I knew what he wanted. Everyone called me Einstein because I'm good at solving problems. But something told me that this would be tougher than anything I'd tackled before. I thought it over. Then I nodded. I'd show Miss Breakbone what a few dunderheads could do.

At breaktime the dunderheads gathered round me.

"It's impossible! She keeps the keys to the drawer on her belt!"

"Then she takes the stuff home!"

"We don't even know where she lives!"

"She reads *Guard Dog Lovers Monthly*!"

I was going to need help.

Lots of it.

At lunch I talked to Wheels.

He's a proper bicycle nut. He put forty-eight extra gears on his bike that summer,

not to mention a reclining seat, indicators, speakers and a water fountain.

He had no problem following Breakbone's car home after school.

He gave me her address. "The place is like a castle! You'll never get in!"

"That's what she thinks," I said. But I needed more info. Then I remembered Pencil.

If she sees something once,

she can draw it from memory.

I sent her off to Breakbone's house.
She drew the outside first.

To get inside, she threw a paper aeroplane over the wall. Breakbone's maid led her through most of the ground floor to get to the backyard.

The map was on my desk by teatime.

By bedtime I'd made a plan.

On Saturday morning I left the house early.

It was time to put the team together.

My first stop was Spider's.

The best way to find him is by looking up. I guess he must have got it from his parents.

"Can you help me out on a little project tonight?"

"What kind of project?"

"One that could seriously damage your health."

"Excellent," he said. "What time?"

I walked round the block to Hollywood's house. She's got every film ever made and has watched them all eleven times. I had a feeling she'd come in handy.

"Are you busy tonight?" I asked.

"It's Saturday, of course I'm busy. I'm going to the cinema, d'uh! Then I'm coming home to watch—"
It took some doing, but I talked her into it.

Spitball was harder to convince.
He used to spit further than anyone
else in school – until a new kid arrived
last spring and beat him by three centimetres.
Spitball was still upset.

"I don't know," he moaned. "What use would I be?" "Plenty," I said. "You'll see." So I signed him up. Followed by the rest of the crew.

Spitball's record

Wheels picked us up at eight o'clock sharp.

When we got there,
we were in luck.
Bad luck. Breakbone
was having a party.

"We're bound to get caught!"

"Let's come back tomorrow!"

"Junkyard needs that cat tomorrow," I said.

"We'll do it tonight." I turned to Spider.

"Check no one's in the backyard."

There was an elm tree on one side of the house.

Spider shot up it.

"All clear," he called down.

I nodded to Clips. He was rubbish at reading.

Even worse at maths. But his paper-clip chains

got ten out of ten...

"Just like you asked for."
He opened his briefcase.
"Two three-metre, eight-strand chains, fisherman's weave with grappling hooks."

We were over the wall in a flash. It was pitch-black. No one could see – except Hollywood. She spent so much time in cinemas, she had perfect night vision. I put her in front.
Suddenly she stopped. "Something's going to happen," she said. "I can tell. Something scary."
"This isn't a film," I said, "it's—"

That's when the four guard dogs charged towards us.
Pencil had told me about them. I looked back
at Junkyard. "Now!"
He whipped out the pork ribs he'd
found in some bin and threw
one to each dog. They stopped
where they were and
started to gnaw.

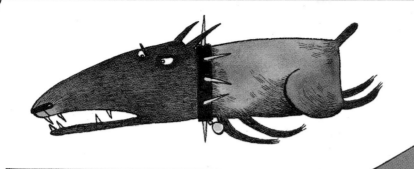

That's when Google-Eyes went to work. Last year she found a book about hypnotism in the library. She put the librarian in a two-week trance. Over the summer she practised lots on her little brother. Those dogs dropped like marionettes.

We slipped into the garage.

"Over here!" said Clips.

And there they were, in a box marked SELL –
the phones and jewellery and iPods, and
everything else Breakbone took that year.
Everything, that is, except the one-eared cat.

"Maybe it's worth something," said Junkyard.
I'd had the same thought already. "I bet she
put it in a safe. We'll need to go in. If only
we knew which room she —"

"Master bedroom," said Hollywood. *"Obviously."*
She was annoying, but she gave good advice.
I studied Pencil's map. "Second floor."

We crept out. Suddenly the security camera
picked us up. I saw Breakbone in the kitchen.
"Spitball – now! Give it everything you've got!"
He popped a piece of bread in his mouth, gave
it a chew, took in a huge breath, then spat
it towards the house.

It shot through th

ght air,

then landed slap-bang
in the middle of the
lens. It was the
greatest feat of
spitting ever seen.
"Nice work," I said.
"The house is full of
people," said Junkyard.
"How do we get in?"

I nodded to Clips. He joined his two chains into one. Spider went up the drainpipe like milk up a straw, then hooked the chain to a second-floor balcony. A minute later, we were inside the house, in a bedroom with sheets on the furniture.

"Must be a guest room," said Clips. "Where's the master bedroom?"

The map only covered the ground floor. But I'd studied the pattern of windows outside and had a rough idea of the layout.

"This way," I said. I opened a door. And there was the party, right below us.

We had to crawl so we wouldn't be seen. Hollywood tugged on my trouser leg. "I'm getting this bad feeling, like something's —"

We crawled down the hall and into a room.
The master bedroom.
"The safe is always behind a painting," said
Hollywood.
I lifted the only painting off the wall. No safe.
"This movie's weird," she said.

"The maid will be back any second," I said. "Everybody look!"

Clips only thinks about paper clips.

He saw one on the floor, bent down to get it, bumped his head on the wall ...

and suddenly that section of wall spun round. There before us was a great big box, bolted to the wall.

"Cool," said Clips.

The box was locked. It was Nails's turn to shine.

He spends a lot of time on his fingernails, filing them into different shapes –

saw blade,

screwdrivers,

letter opener

and keys.

Unfortunately, none of them fitted the lock. Fortunately, he keeps one nail long and untouched, just for occasions like this. With his clipper and file, he turned it into a custom key.

The box opened. And there was the cat.
"Back to your owner," I said. I tossed it to
Junkyard and dropped a little something in
its place. "Now let's get out of here."

Then the bedroom door opened. And there stood the maid.

She was so frightened that nothing came out when she tried to scream. Spider pulled her in and shut the door. Google-Eyes jumped up on the bed, put her face in front of the maid's and gave her the Express Trance. Five seconds later the maid fell backwards.

"Let's go," I said. We went out the way we came in. Wheels was waiting outside. Junkyard's smile told him the mission had been a success.

On Sunday Junkyard's mum
received the one-eared cat.

Those strange green
eyes turned out to
be emeralds. Worth a
lot of money.
To say thank you, Junkyard's
mum gave him a voucher for unlimited ice cream.
He invited me to the ice cream shop with him.

"There's just one thing I've been wondering," he said. "What did you put in Breakbone's box?"

"Just a little note to our teacher," I replied.